SING-ALONG
ALEF
BET

Based on the song by
Mama Doni and Eric Lindberg

Illustrations by Rinat Gilboa

APPLES & HONEY PRESS

Springfield, NJ • Jerusalem

Sing-Along Alef Bet is dedicated to our families:
the Zasloffs, and the Lindbergs,
and of course to Millie and Xander.

Millie and Xander: We hope that this song and book will be passed on for
generations to come in our family. We hope that you will keep this book by
your bed and know it and love it. And that you will pass it on to your children
someday, and that they will pass it on to their children, and to their children,
and to theirs. May you always cherish these Hebrew letters with all of your
hearts and always be proud of who you are.
—Doni & Eric

For my parents, who were the first to teach me the alef bet.
—Rinat

Apples & Honey Press
An imprint of Behrman House and Gefen Publishing House
Behrman House, 11 Edison Place, Springfield, New Jersey 07081
Gefen Publishing House Ltd, 6 Hatzvi Street, Jerusalem 94386, Israel
www.applesandhoneypress.com

Text copyright © 2016 by Doni Zasloff and Eric Lindberg
Illustrations copyright © 2016 by Rinat Gilboa

ISBN 978-1-68115-509-8

Library of Congress Cataloging-in-Publication Data

Zasloff, Doni.
Sing-along alef bet / by Mama Doni & Eric Lindberg ; illustrations by Rinat Gilboa.
pages cm
ISBN 978-1-68115-509-8
1. Children's songs, English—United States--Texts. [1. Hebrew language—Alphabet. 2. Alphabet.
3. Songs.] I. Lindberg, Eric. II. Gilboa, Rinat, illustrator. III. Title.
PZ8.3.T311Si 2016
782.42—dc23
[E]
2015007964

Design by Elynn Cohen and Rinat Gilboa
Edited by Ann D. Koffsky

Do you know the **alef bet**? I do!

Alef is for **aba** and **ima**.
That's a dad and mom.

Bet is my **bayit**,
at home where I belong.

Vet is in **ahavah**.
That's our word for love.

Gimmel is **gibor/giborah**,
our heroes we're proud of.

Dalet is for **delet**,
the door into my room.

הַלְלוּיָהּ

Hay is **halleluyah**!
What I say when
I see you!

Vav is for **vered**,
a sweet-smelling rose.

Zayin is **zahav**.
That zayin word means gold.

Chet is for my **challah**,
my favorite kind of bread.

Tet is **tipah**,
a raindrop on my head.

Yud is for **yarei'ach,**
the moon up in the sky.

Kaf is for my **kelev**.
My dog by my side.

Chaf is in **b'rachah**,
the blessing that
we say.

Lamed is for **lailah**, when nighttime comes our way.

Mem is for matzah.

Nun for na'al—
that's my shoe.

Samech is for **sus**.
That means horse
in Hebrew.

Ayin is for **eitz**,
the tree that
grows so high.

Pay is for **parpar**.
I love the butterfly.

Fay is in my **sefer**,
the book that I read.

Tzadi's for **tzedakah**
we give to those
in need.

Kuf is for my **kol**,
my voice that
sings this song.

Reish is for my **rosh**.
My head knows
right from wrong.

רֹאשׁ

Shin is for **Shabbat**.
I finally get a break.

Tav is for the **Torah**,
how we live and learn.

Now we know our **alef bet**.

Now try it. It's your turn!

Dear Friends,

Being Jewish is so many things! From eating challah on Shabbat, to lighting candles on Hanukkah; from spending time with family, to singing your heart out with so much RU'ACH (spirit), many of our joyful life experiences are Jewish ones.

The Hebrew language is a big part of Jewish life, and many Jews all over the world know the *alef bet*. We may speak different languages in our day-to-day lives and come from varied backgrounds, but the Hebrew letters touch all our hearts.

When we sing from our prayer books or chant from the Torah, it's the alef bet at the core of the experience. Hebrew is the tie, the glue that holds Jews together around the world. These aren't just letters . . . these letters connect us to one another.

Ask your children, "What are your favorite Hebrew words from this book?" Then, try using the words in a sentence. For example, "Look at the *yarei'ach* (moon)." Or, "Don't forget to feed the *kelev* (dog)." Invite your children to create their own sentences, too.

Music can bring Hebrew to life! Ask your children what prayer or Hebrew song they like the most, and why. When was the first time they remember hearing or singing something in Hebrew?

Learn "The Alef Bet Song" that's in this book by downloading the free app at www.applesandhoneypress.com. Using the app, your children can listen to the song and record themselves singing along with our Mama Doni Band. Sing with them!

Sending lots of love to you and your *mishpachah* (family)!

B'ahavah (with love),

Doni Zasloff and Eric Lindberg